This book belongs to :

K McLean

....

The Midsummer Banquet

Written & Illustrated by
John Patience

PUBLISHED BY PETER HADDOCK LIMITED, BRIDLINGTON, ENGLAND.
© FERN HOLLOW PRODUCTIONS LIMITED
PRINTED IN ITALY
ISBN 0-7105-0333-4

In a few days it would be time for the Midsummer Banquet
to be held at Trundleberry Manor. In his attic, Lord Trundle
was rummaging around looking for the candelabras and
punch bowl which he had stored away after the previous
year's celebrations.

"Now, where did I put them," he muttered, "perhaps they
are in this chest."

Opening the chest, he found, amongst many other things, an
old engraving of a medieval castle — FERN HOLLOW CASTLE!

"That's rather odd," muttered Lord Trundle. "There's no
castle in Fern Hollow these days. It must have fallen into
ruins many years ago. But this gives me an idea. This year we
will have a medieval Midsummer Banquet and everyone can
come in medieval costume."

Lord Trundle lost no time in sending out the invitations and soon everyone in the village was talking about the banquet. Mr. and Mrs. Thimble, the Fern Hollow Tailors, were kept extremely busy making the medieval costumes and the lights in their windows burned late into the night. When at last the clothes were finished the animals came to try them on. You would hardly have recognised Brock Gruffy, Mr. Bouncer or Mrs. Willowbank in their costumes. They looked splendid!

The morning before the banquet Lord Trundle decided that he would visit Mr. Crackleberry who would be doing the catering. He was driving along in his car when a thick mist came down. Unable to see where he was going, and still thinking that he was on the road, he drove down a narrow track into Windy Wood. After some time the track petered out and Lord Trundle's car got stuck in the mud. Then the poor fox had to get out and struggle along on foot. Suddenly the mist began to clear and, to his surprise, Lord Trundle found himself standing in front of Fern Hollow Castle.

It was the same castle as the one in Lord Trundle's engraving. Although it was mostly in ruins, one of the towers was still standing and naturally the fox felt that he must explore it. As he climbed the stone staircase inside the tower,

Lord Trundle's footsteps echoed noisily, disturbing some bats which fluttered around his head. They gave him quite a fright. At the top of the stairs was a heavy wooden door. He opened it and entered a dusty little room filled with suits of armour and other interesting things. Suddenly a gust of wind blew in through the window and slammed the door shut. Lord Trundle tried to open it but it was locked. He was trapped!

As soon as it was realised that Lord Trundle was missing, P.C. Hoppit organised a search party to find him. The clever policeman quickly deduced what had happened and the search party followed the tracks of Lord Trundle's car into Windy Wood. When at last they arrived at the Castle, they found the fox waving from the Castle window and shouting for help.

The search party had come well-equipped and a length of
strong rope was quickly thrown up to Lord Trundle.
"Tie one end of it to the door handle," instructed
P.C. Hoppit, "then climb down."
Lord Trundle was not accustomed to climbing down ropes
but, with the encouragement of his friends, he managed to
lower himself safely down to the ground. When he had
recovered from his ordeal he announced that he had had a
brilliant idea.
"Let's hold the Midsummer Banquet here at the Castle,"
he said.
"It's the perfect place for it."

A great deal of work was put into the preparations for the banquet. Lots of fairy lights were hung in the trees around the Castle and Mr. Chips made an enormous wooden table, big enough for all the animals to sit around. On the night of the banquet everyone turned up in their medieval costumes, carrying lanterns. There was even medieval music supplied by Sigmund Swamp, who played a lute and sang a few little songs which he had written.

Finally, an enormous bonfire was lit and there was a wonderful firework display, with rockets flying up into the night sky to burst into flowers of coloured sparks above the ruins of the Castle. It was a really wonderful evening, one which the Fern Hollow animals would remember for a long, long time.

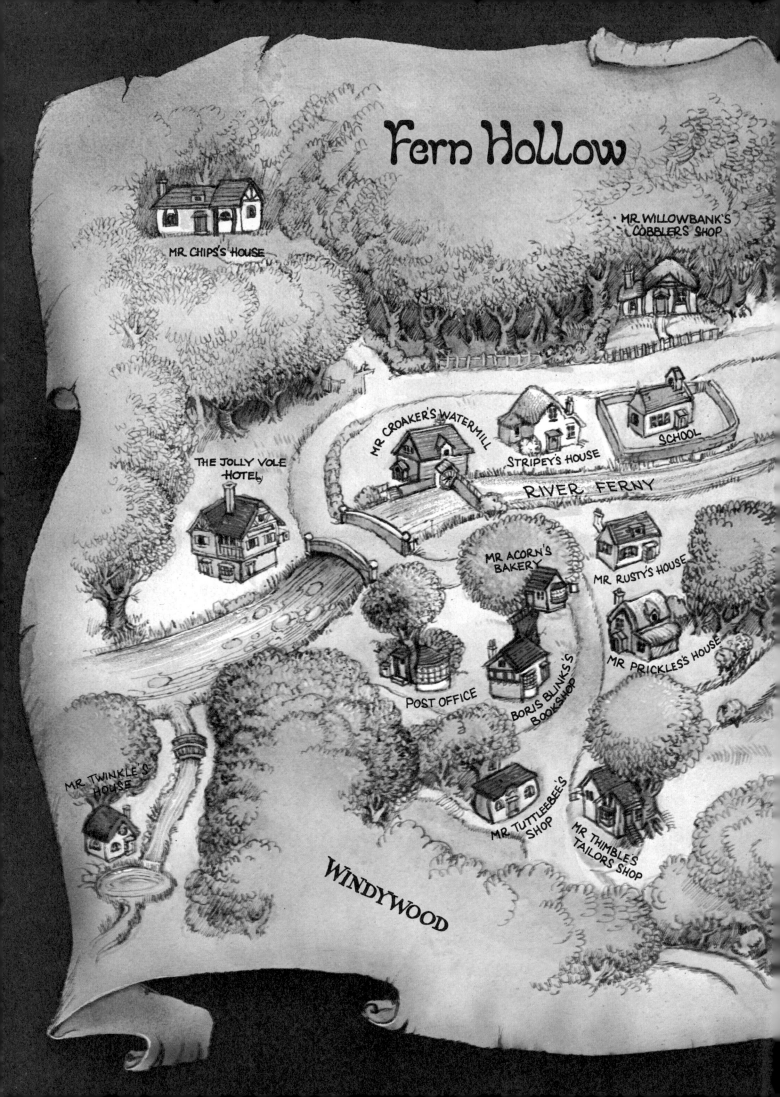